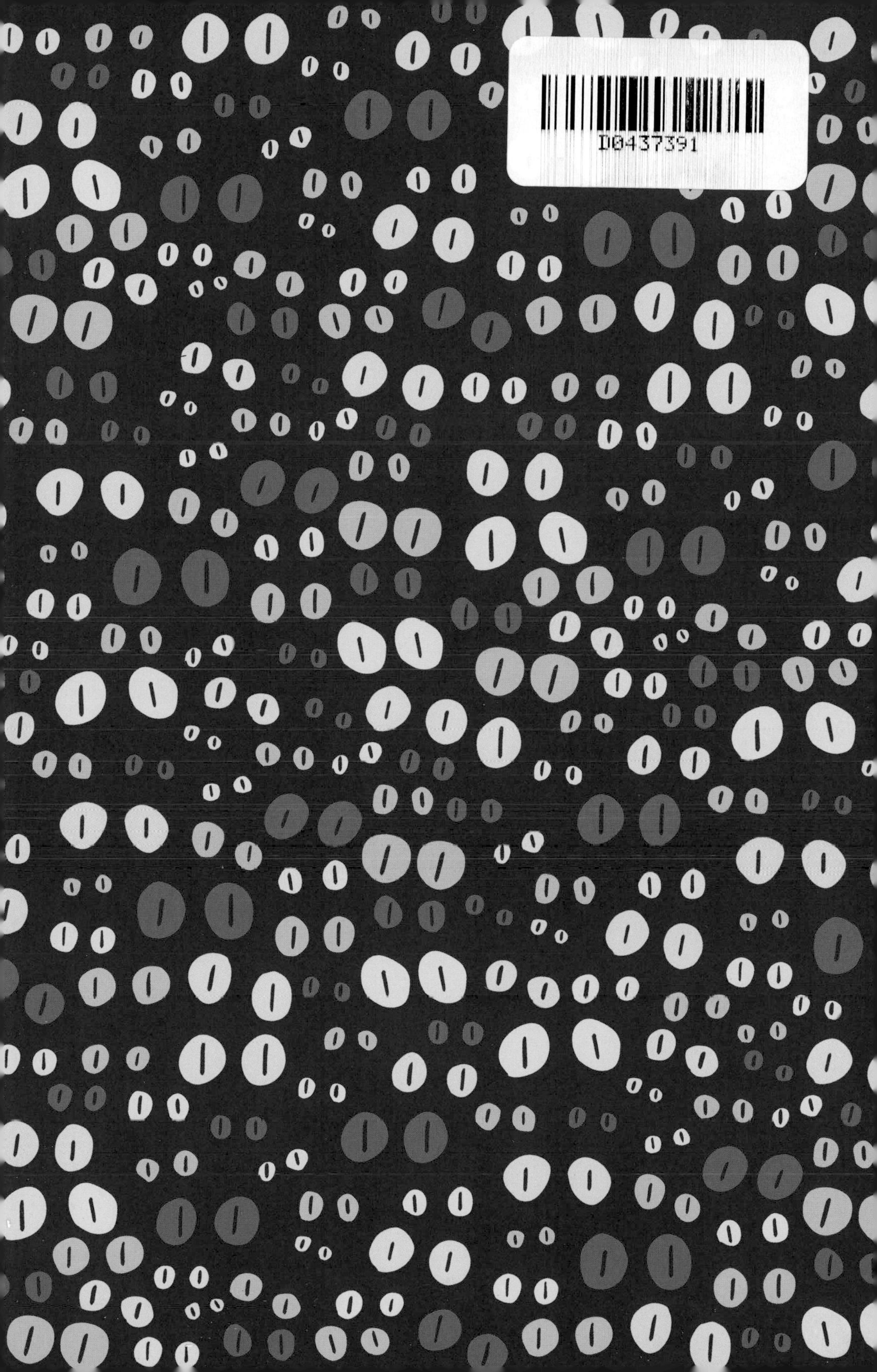
D0437391

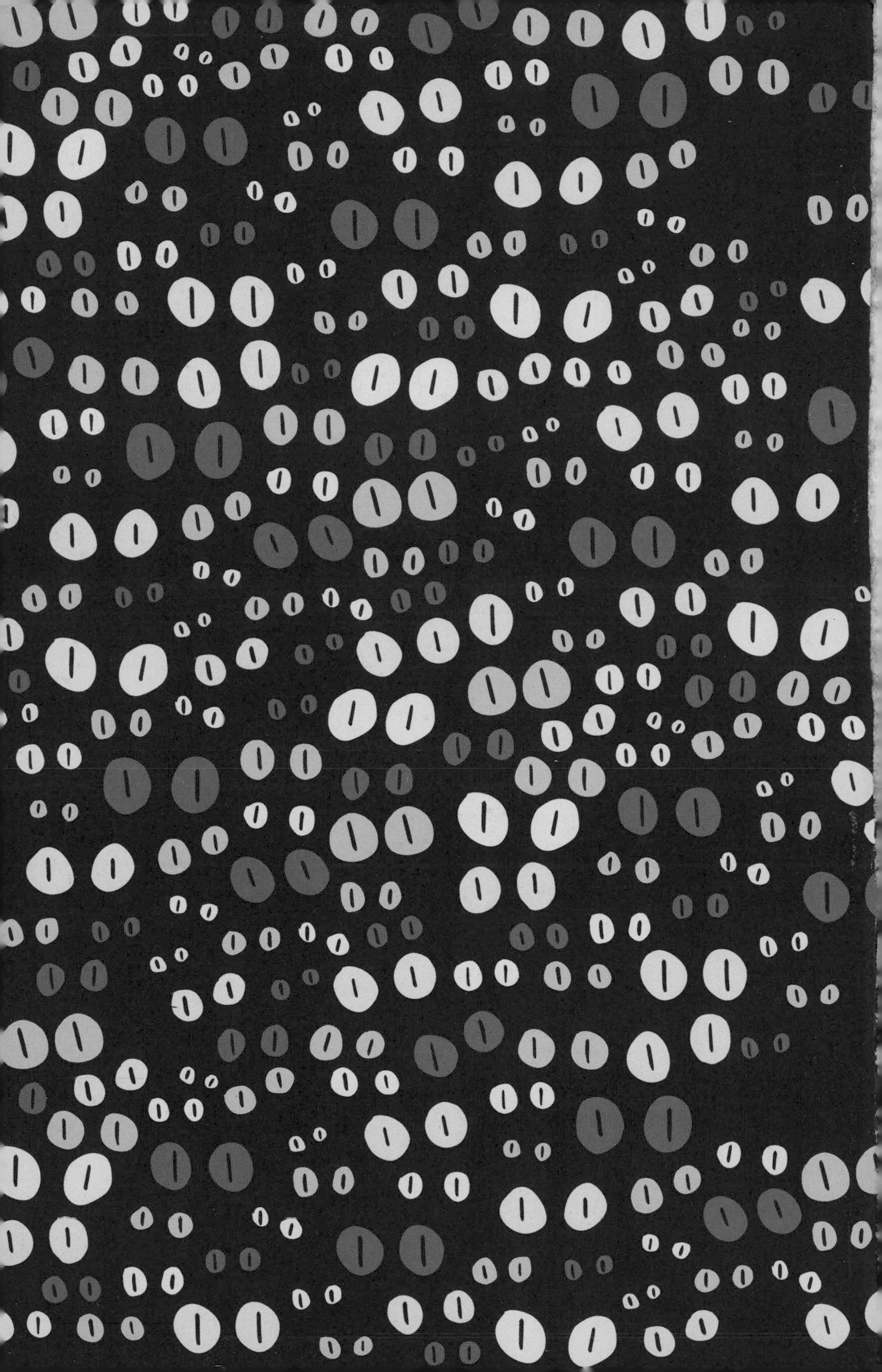

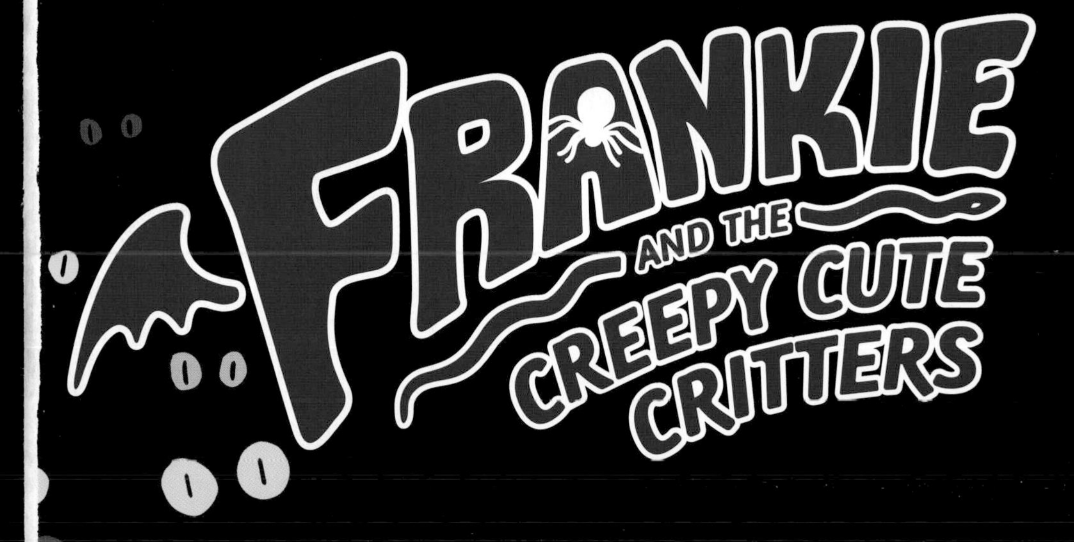

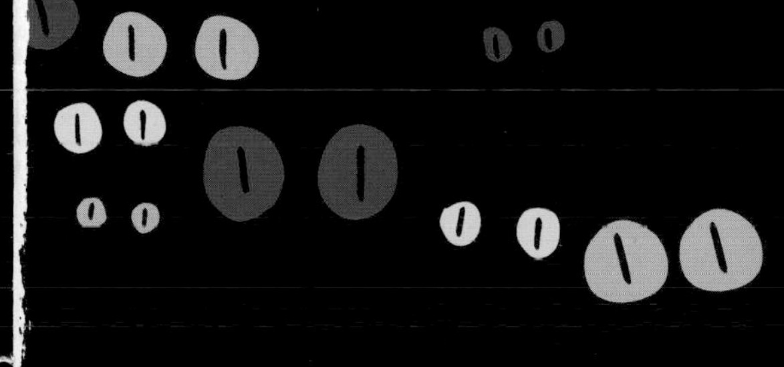

AN ONI PRESS PUBLICATION

Written and illustrated by
CAITLIN ROSE BOYLE
Lettered by
TOM B. LONG

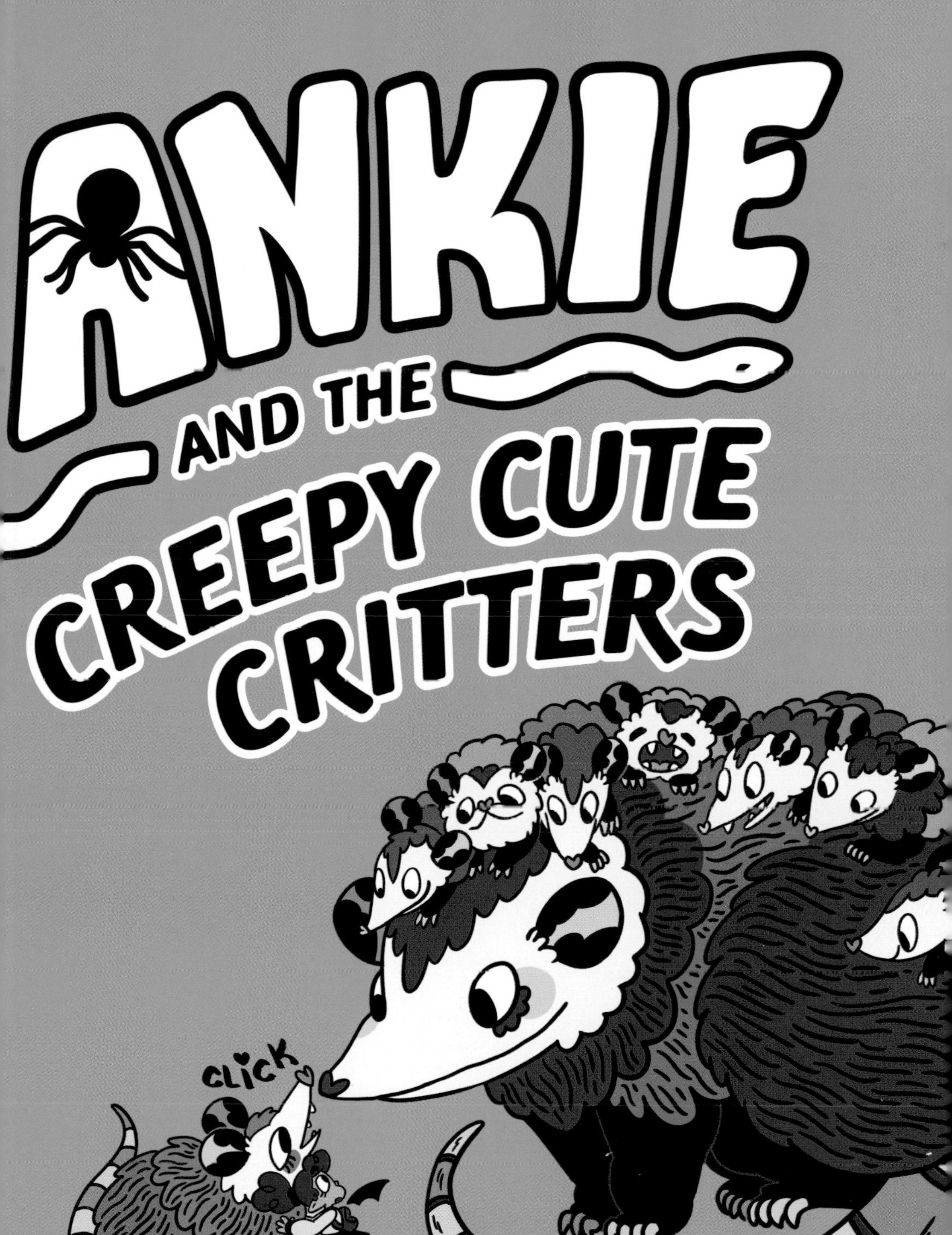
ANKIE
AND THE
CREEPY CUTE
CRITTERS
CLICK

Edited by **ROBIN HERRERA**
with assistance from **SARAH GAYDOS**
Designed by **KATE Z. STONE**

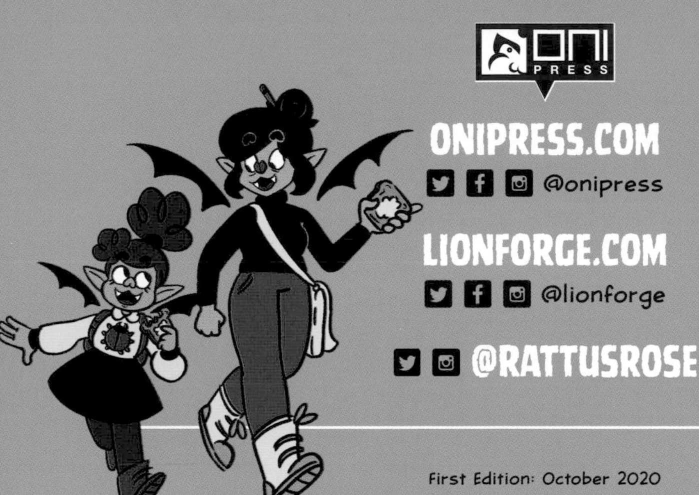

ONIPRESS.COM
@onipress

LIONFORGE.COM
@lionforge

@RATTUSROSE

First Edition: October 2020
ISBN 978-1-62010-782-9
eISBN 978-1-62010-803-1

FRANKIE AND THE CREEPY CUTE CRITTERS, October 2020. Published by Oni-Lion Forge Publishing Group, LLC, 1319 SE Martin Luther King Jr. Blvd., Suite 240, Portland, OR 97214.

Printed in China.

Library of Congress Control Number: 2020934255

10 9 8 7 6 5 4 3 2 1

FOR EMERY

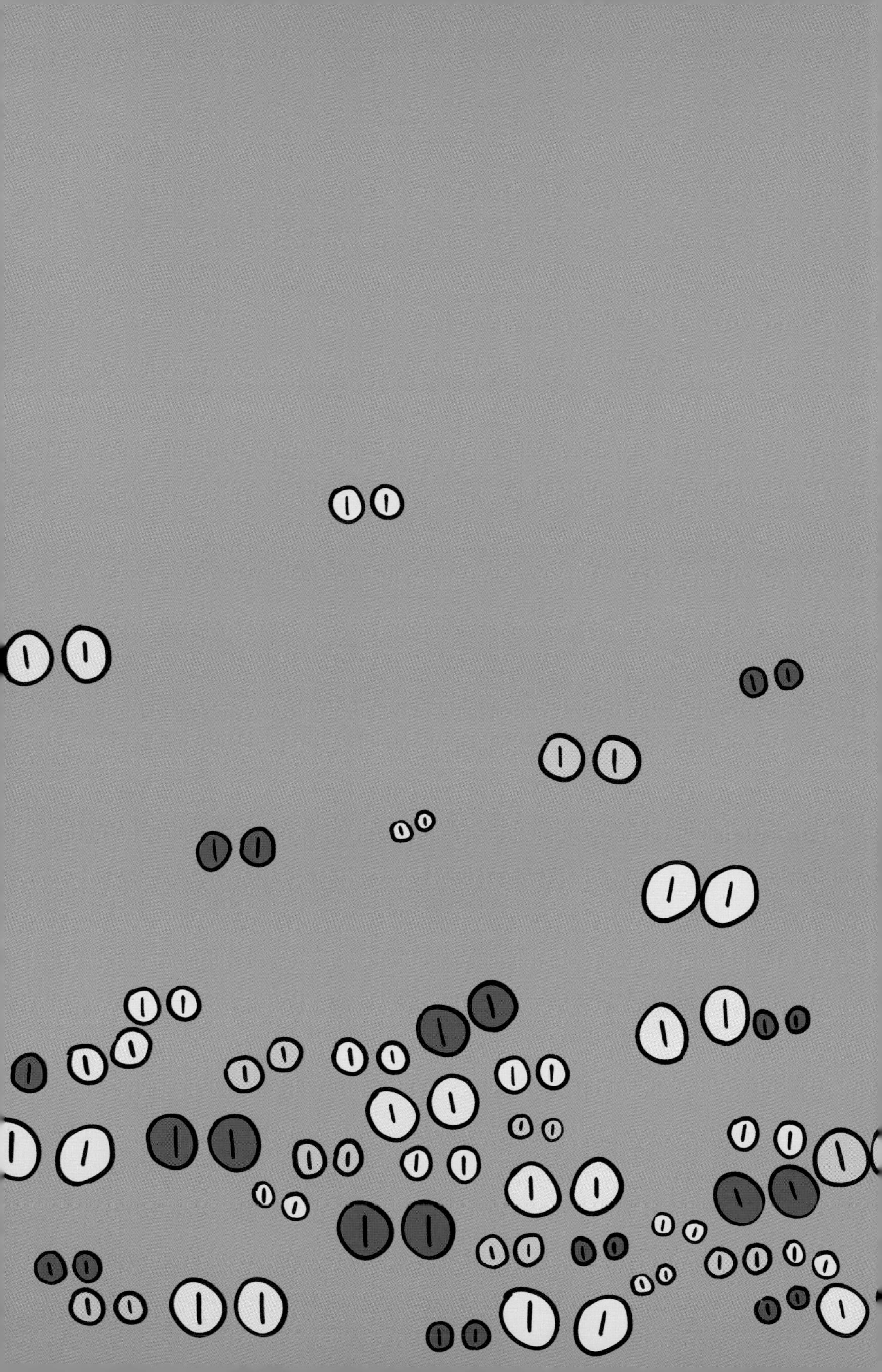

BAT FACES

tik tik tik tik tik tik

DING!
EEK! EEK! EE

EEK! EEK! EEK! EEK!
GASP!

EEK! EEK

EEK! EEK!

EEK! EEK!
YAWN!

SQUEAAAAAAK
CLICK
OH FRAAAAAAANKIE...
COME ON, SLEEPYHEAD, TIME TO GET MOVING.
CLICK
SO FUSSY! IF YOU STAY IN BED MUCH LONGER, WE'LL BOTH BE LATE FOR CLASS.
HHHISSSSS
WAIT... CLASS?
DID I FORGET TO TELL YOU SCHOOL STARTS TODAY? I GUESS YOU CAN JUST STAY HOME....
NONONO! I'M UP! I'LL GO GET READY!
ZOOOM!!!

BRUSHABRUSH
FLOOF
YANK
MOOOOOOMMMM! I'M READYYYYYYY!
DO YOU HAVE EVERYTHING YOU NEED FOR SCHOOL?
YES!
NOTEBOOKS? PENCILS? PENCIL TOP ERASERS SHAPED LIKE TINY RAINBOW SPIDERS?
OF COURSE! I WOULDN'T FORGET THE ESSENTIALS!
I DO KNOW ONE THING YOU FORGOT....
BREAKFAST!

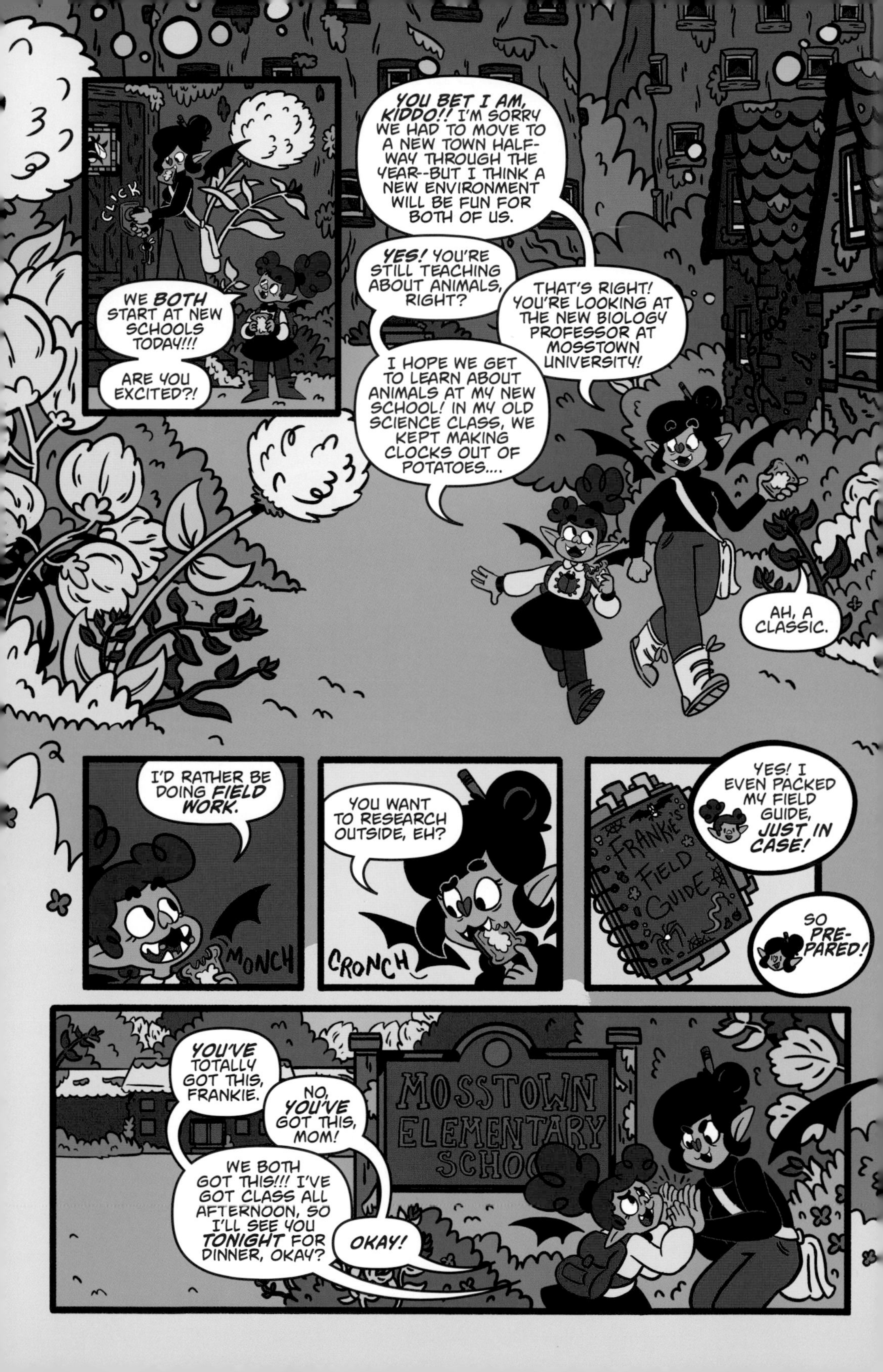
CLICK
WE BOTH START AT NEW SCHOOLS TODAY!!!
ARE YOU EXCITED?!
YES! YOU'RE STILL TEACHING ABOUT ANIMALS, RIGHT?
YOU BET I AM, KIDDO!! I'M SORRY WE HAD TO MOVE TO A NEW TOWN HALF-WAY THROUGH THE YEAR--BUT I THINK A NEW ENVIRONMENT WILL BE FUN FOR BOTH OF US.
THAT'S RIGHT! YOU'RE LOOKING AT THE NEW BIOLOGY PROFESSOR AT MOSSTOWN UNIVERSITY!
I HOPE WE GET TO LEARN ABOUT ANIMALS AT MY NEW SCHOOL! IN MY OLD SCIENCE CLASS, WE KEPT MAKING CLOCKS OUT OF POTATOES....
AH, A CLASSIC.
I'D RATHER BE DOING FIELD WORK.
MONCH
YOU WANT TO RESEARCH OUTSIDE, EH?
CRONCH
FRANKIE'S FIELD GUIDE
YES! I EVEN PACKED MY FIELD GUIDE, JUST IN CASE!
SO PRE-PARED!
MOSSTOWN ELEMENTARY SCHO
YOU'VE TOTALLY GOT THIS, FRANKIE.
NO, YOU'VE GOT THIS, MOM!
WE BOTH GOT THIS!!! I'VE GOT CLASS ALL AFTERNOON, SO I'LL SEE YOU TONIGHT FOR DINNER, OKAY?
OKAY!

HI!!!
I'M FRANKIE, AND I'M NEW HERE!

WHAT ARE YOUR NAMES??? WHAT'S YOUR FAVORITE CLASS?

WHAT'S YOUR FAVORITE BUG??? MINE'S THE LUNA...
FLINCH!

...MOTH...
HMM... MAYBE THEY DON'T LIKE BUGS?

WHISPER
WHISPER
WHISPER
WHISPER
DID YOU SEE THE NEW FAIRY?
HER TEETH ARE SO SHARP AND SCARY....
HER VOICE! IT'S SO LOW AND CREEPY!

...HER WINGS ARE ALL LEATHERY....

SHE'S SO SCARY!

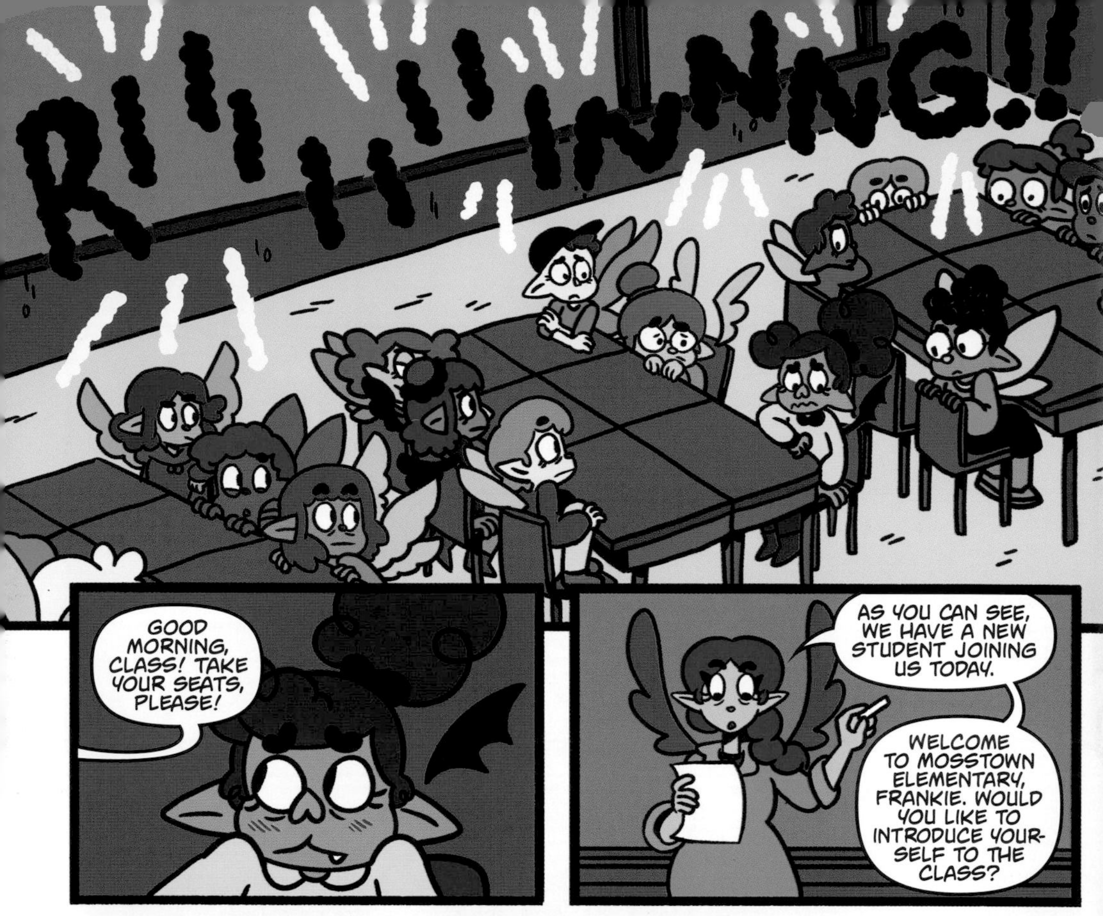

GOOD MORNING, CLASS! TAKE YOUR SEATS, PLEASE!

AS YOU CAN SEE, WE HAVE A NEW STUDENT JOINING US TODAY.

WELCOME TO MOSSTOWN ELEMENTARY, FRANKIE. WOULD YOU LIKE TO INTRODUCE YOURSELF TO THE CLASS?

HIII EVERYBODY....
I'M FRANKIE FAIRY... I LIKE NATURE WALKS AND WRITING IN MY FIELD GUIDE....
MORE LIKE FRANKIE SCARY!!!

SO SCARY! AND CREEPY!
DO YOU THINK SHE BITES?
EVERYBODY, PLEASE! SETTLE DOWN, SETTLE DOWN....

RIIIIIIIINNG!!!
YAAAAAY
RACE YOU HOME!
HEHEHEHEHEHE
YOU'RE ON!
HAHAHAHAHAHA
MOOOOMMMMMM! I'M HOMEEE!
AWW, HEY TUNA.
MOOOM?

FRANKIE-
I have class all afternoon, but I'll be home for dinner!
♥ Mom
OH... THAT'S RIGHT.
RRROWWWRRR?

WANNA GO FOR A WALK, GIRL?
RWOWR!

WELL....
CLICK
MAYBE SOME FIELD WORK WILL CHEER ME UP.
WE CAN ADD MOSSTOWN TO THE GUIDE.
MROWR!

THE LOCAL PLANTS SEEM... *FINE.*
CRABGRASS FINE, DANDELIONS, BORING BUT *FINE.*

LOCAL ROCKS ARE *UNREMARKABLE.*
SNIF SNUF

SCH
SCHOOL: FULL OF *WHISPERING JERKS.*

THE PUDDLES? *STINKY.*
SPLISH!

MOSSTOWN'S *NOT A GOOD PLACE TO LIVE.*
IT'S NOT INTERESTING. IT'S NOT WORTH WRITING IN MY FIELD GUIDE ABOUT....

EVEN THE *NATURE'S* BORING!
IT'S JUST A BUNCH OF *WEEDS.*
A BUNCH OF WEEDS, AND *ME...*
SNIF SNUF

...ME...
SCARY FAIRY
SCRIBBLE
...FRANKIE, THE SCARY FAIRY.
WOOOOOO
OOAAAAAAA
WAF WAF WAF WA
AHOOOF!
WUMPH!
TUNA!!!! TUNA, NO, COME BACK, GIRL!
GRRRRRRRRRRR
THAT'S A...
...SNAKE!!!!!!

YAWN

FLICK
SCOOT
GRRRRRR
SLITHER SLITHER
OH! OKAY...
BYE, THEN!

I THINK THAT WAS... A GARTER SNAKE?
NOT A GOOD PLACE TO SIT. OOPS.
BUT WHERE IS IT GOING...?

OH! THEY'RE NAPPING IN THE SUN!
IT'S A LITTLE CHILLY TODAY-- I BET THE SUN ON THE ROCKS FEELS NICE AND WARM!

WHERE'S MY GARTER SNAKE PAGE...?
GARTER SNAKE
A COMMON BACKYARD SNAKE
•LEAVE THEM ALONE AND THEY WON'T BOTHER YOU!
•THEY HAVE OTHER COLORS DEPENDING ON WHERE THEY LIVE.
EASTERN GARTER SNAKE
WE SAW THIS KIND.
SNAKES HAVE COLD BLOOD.
THIS MEANS THEY CAN'T STAY WARM WITHOUT HELP FROM THE SUN.
SUN
SO WHEN YOU SEE A SNAKE IN THE SUN, THEY'RE WARMING UP!
HEAT
WHEN SNAKES DO THIS, IT'S CALLED
BASKING
THAT YAWN WAS SCARY! I WONDER IF THAT'S WHAT I LOOK LIKE IN THE MORNING....

ANY OTHER SNAKE FACTS IN HERE?
FLIP!

SNAKES YAWN TO ADJUST THEIR JAW BEFORE OR AFTER EATING.
ribbit

LET'SSSSS GET BACK TO OUR WALK, HUH, TUNA?
SNAP!

DIG DIG

MOSSTOWN IS ACTUALLY PRETTY COOL!
I'M ADDING SO MANY NEW PAGES TO THE GUIDE... WE EXPLORED SO MUCH ALREADY!
I CAN'T WAIT TO SHOW MOM!
LET'S REST UP FOR A BIT BEFORE WE HEAD BACK. READY FOR A SNACK BREAK, TUNA?
BORK BORK!

I KNOW THE SNACKS ARE IN HERE SOMEWHERE....
CLICK
CLICK
CREAK
SNAP
CLICK
WHINE
SNAP
CLICK
CLICK
CLICK

CLICK SNAP CLICK CLICK
WHEEZE
SOME-THING'S IN THE GRASS OVER THERE...
...SOMETHING THAT SOUNDS AWFUL.
IS THERE AN ANIMAL THAT CLICKS AND HISSES?
CLICK SNAP CLICK SNAP
WHIIIIINEEE
I'M JUST GOING TO TAKE A QUICK PEEK... AND THEN WE CAN GO HOME...
WHEEZE
WHEEZE

rustle
rustle
CLICK CLICK CLICK CLICK CLICK CLICK
BABY POSSUM???
CLICK?

EEEEEEEEEEEEEEE
FLOP!

HOW DID THIS HAPPEN! I SCARED IT SO BADLY IT ***DIED?*** I ONLY WANTED TO TAKE A PEEK....
AM I REALLY ***THAT*** SCARY...???
TUP TUP TUP

WAIT A MINUTE... CAN DEAD ANIMALS ***BREATHE?***
MY GUIDE SAYS THAT POSSUMS ***PLAY DEAD*** WHEN THEY'RE ***SCARED!!!***
SNIF
AND BABIES ARE KIND OF ***BAD*** AT IT! AWW, YOU TRIED, BABY!
TWITCH!

SORRY ABOUT THAT, BABY. I GUESS I DID SCARE YOU AS MUCH AS YOUR NOISES SCARED ME!
I'LL MAKE IT UP TO YOU.
HERE...
SNIF

...HAVE A SNACK!

MONCH!

YAY!!!! POSSUMS LIKE STRAW-BERRIES! WHAT A GOOD SCIENTIFIC DISCOVERY!
MONCH MONCH MONCH
WE HAVE TO ADD THAT TO THE FIELD GUIDE.

YOU POOR BITEY BABY... WHY ARE YOU ALL ALONE? WILL YOU BE OKAY IF I LEAVE YOU HERE?
MUNCH MUNCH MUNCH
I REALLY DO HAVE TO GO HOME SOON....

THAT WAS A LOUD ONE....
CLICK
K
CLICK
BITEY, NO!
DO YOU WANT ANOTHER STRAWBERRY? HERE, GIRL!
BITEY, WHATEVER'S CLACKING IS GOING TO FIND US....

AHH!
CLACK SLACK
rustle
CLACK CLACK
rustle

CLICK
BITEY, RUN! IT'S COMING!!!
YOU HAVE TO RUN!

I'LL PROTECT YOU FROM...
CLACK

...YOUR... MOM?
BITEY, WERE YOU CALLING FOR YOUR FAMILY?
CLICK

THE SCARY NOISES WERE YOU TWO TRYING TO FIND EACH OTHER! YOU WERE JUST TALKING!

HOP!

YOU'RE ALL PRETTY CUTE WHEN YOU AREN'T YELLING.

MY MOM IS GOING TO START CLICK-CLACKING AFTER ME IF I DON'T HURRY HOME SOON....
CLASSES MUST BE JUST ABOUT OVER.

WHOA THERE, MOMMA POSSUM!
HOP!
TOSS!
I GUESS... WE'RE GETTING A RIDE!
I'VE NEVER TRAVELED BY POSSUM BEFORE!
TRUNDLE TRUNDLE

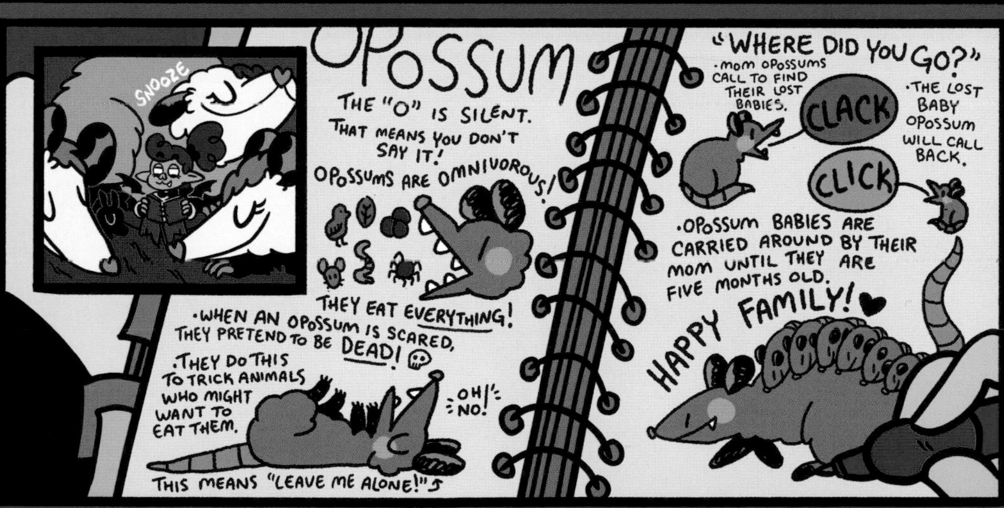
SNOOZE
OPOSSUM
THE "O" IS SILENT. THAT MEANS YOU DON'T SAY IT!
OPOSSUMS ARE OMNIVOROUS!
THEY EAT EVERYTHING!
•WHEN AN OPOSSUM IS SCARED, THEY PRETEND TO BE DEAD!
•THEY DO THIS TO TRICK ANIMALS WHO MIGHT WANT TO EAT THEM.
OH! NO!
THIS MEANS "LEAVE ME ALONE!"
"WHERE DID YOU GO?"
•MOM OPOSSUMS CALL TO FIND THEIR LOST BABIES.
CLACK
•THE LOST BABY OPOSSUM WILL CALL BACK.
CLICK
•OPOSSUM BABIES ARE CARRIED AROUND BY THEIR MOM UNTIL THEY ARE FIVE MONTHS OLD.
HAPPY FAMILY!

CLICK
CLICK
CLICK
CLICK
THANK YOU, MOMMA POSSUM! THANKS, BITEY, THANKS, BABIES! HAVE A SAFE TRIP HOME!
I'LL ALWAYS REMEMBER YOUR YELLING, AND THE WAY YOU CHOMPED THAT STRAWBERRY!!!!

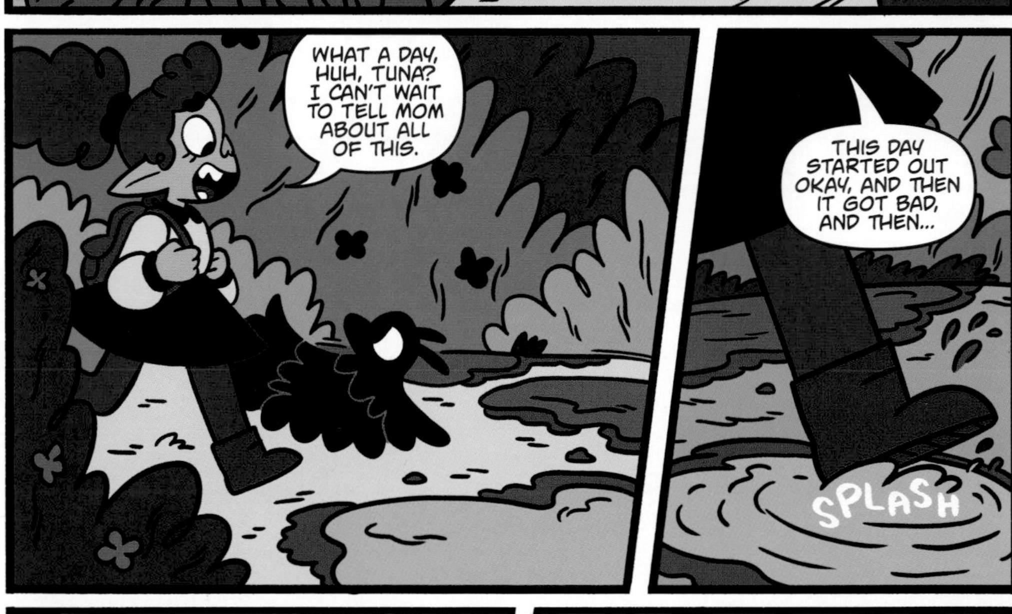
WHAT A DAY, HUH, TUNA? I CAN'T WAIT TO TELL MOM ABOUT ALL OF THIS.
THIS DAY STARTED OUT OKAY, AND THEN IT GOT BAD, AND THEN...
SPLASH

...IT GOT A LITTLE SCARY...
BUZZ
BUZZ
BUZZ
BUZZ
...BUT IT TURNED OUT ALRIGHT IN THE END!
...DO YOU HEAR SOMETHING, TUNA?

BZZZZZZZZZZZZZZZZZ
OH! MORE WILDLIFE!
I THINK THOSE ARE MOSQUITOES....

I WONDER WHAT MY MOSQUITO PAGE SAYS....
WHINE!
OWW!

MAYBE NOW IS NOT A "RESEARCH" TIME...
BORK

...MAYBE NOW IT'S TIME TO RUN!

OH, TUNA!!!
DASH
I KNOW NOT ALL SCARY ANIMALS ARE BAD...
HOP
...BUT MAYBE MOSQUITOS ARE JUST MEANIES!
DASH
I CAN'T RUN MUCH FARTHER, TUNA...
...BUT I DON'T HEAR THE MOSQUITOES?
AND IT'S EVEN DARKER NOW??
PHEW
BORK
HOW...?

CRUNCH
OH!!!
BATS!!!

AAAAAAAHHH

CHOMP!

PHEW. IT'S DINNERTIME FOR THEM TOO, I GUESS.

ENJOY YOUR MEAL! AND THANK YOUUUUU!

LITTLE BROWN
BAT
• A FLYING MAMMAL!
• BATS ARE NOCTURNAL.
• THEY SLEEP DURING THE DAY AND ARE AWAKE AT NIGHT!
THEY SLEEP UPSIDE-DOWN!
ZZZ
BATS EAT BUGS
THEY HUNT BY ECHOLOCATING. THIS MEANS THEY CALL OUT TO THEIR SURROUNDINGS...
YELL
...AND THEY LISTEN FOR THE CALLS TO BOUNCE BACK.
ECHO

SCRIBBLE
SCRIBBLE

SIGH

HELLOOOOOO! FRANKIE?
IN HERE, MOM!

DINNER'S READY!
...AND THEN THE BATS ATE ALL OF THE MOSQUITOES!!!
THEY SAVED ME!
THE MOM SIDE OF ME IS VERY STRESSED OUT BY THIS STORY, BUT THE SCIENTIST IN ME IS SO EXCITED TO HEAR ABOUT ALL THE FIELD RESEARCH YOU DID TODAY!
TACO
TUNA
SO YOU SAW A SNAKE, A FAMILY OF POSSUMS, A BUNCH OF BATS, AND ALL SORTS OF OTHER CREEPY CRITTERS! BUT TELL ME, HOW WAS SCHOOL?

WELL....

MOM... AM I SCARY?
WHAT DO YOU MEAN, FRANKIE?

THE KIDS AT SCHOOL SAID I WAS CREEPY... NOBODY WANTED TO TALK TO ME. THEY CALLED ME FRANKIE SCARY.
AH, FRANKIE. I'M SO SORRY.

BUT BEING SCARY ISN'T ALWAYS A BAD THING.

HAVING SHARP TEETH, OR MAKING CREEPY NOISES, THESE THINGS SERVE A PURPOSE....

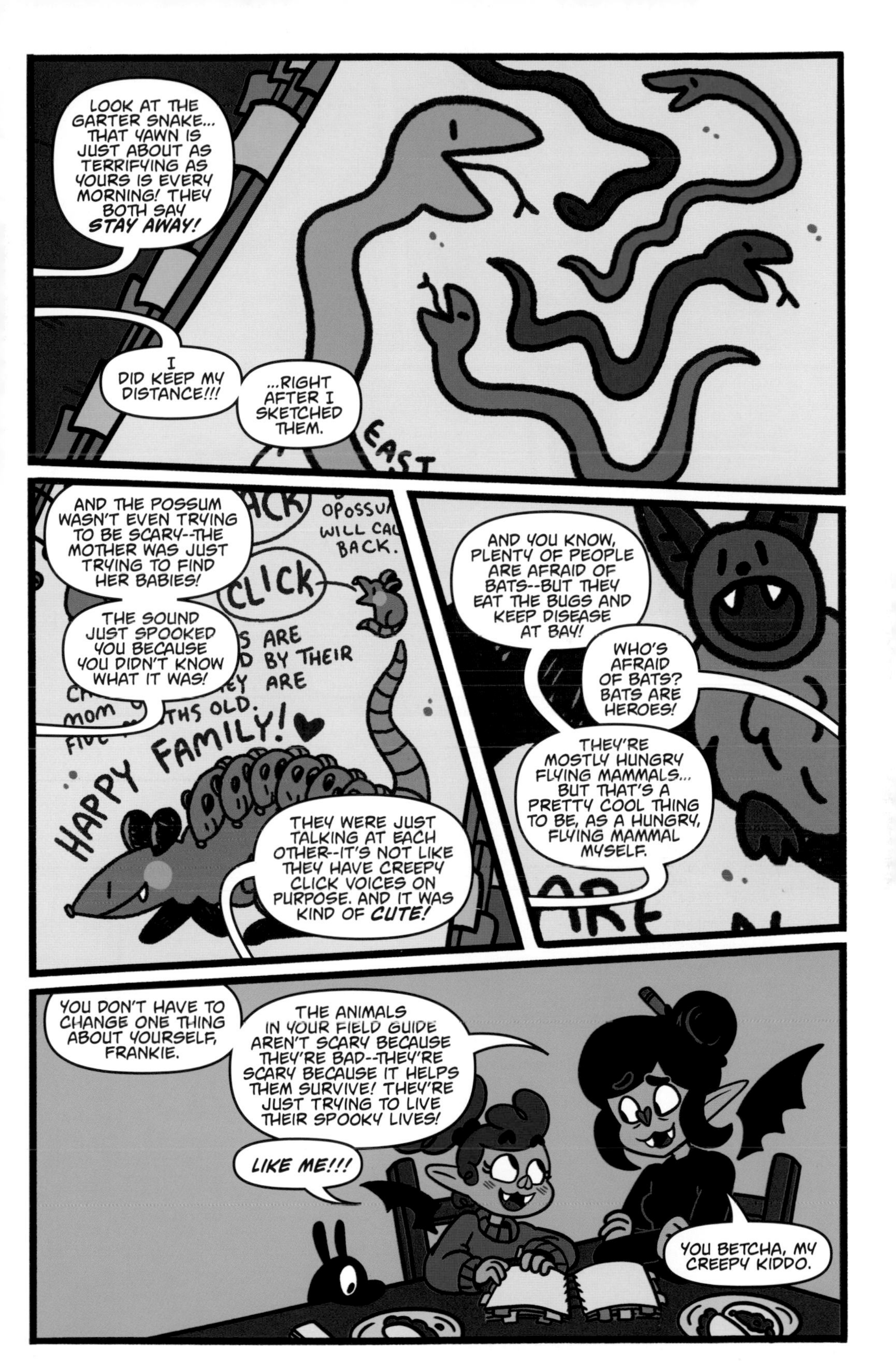
LOOK AT THE GARTER SNAKE... THAT YAWN IS JUST ABOUT AS TERRIFYING AS YOURS IS EVERY MORNING! THEY BOTH SAY STAY AWAY!
I DID KEEP MY DISTANCE!!!
...RIGHT AFTER I SKETCHED THEM.
EAST
AND THE POSSUM WASN'T EVEN TRYING TO BE SCARY--THE MOTHER WAS JUST TRYING TO FIND HER BABIES!
THE SOUND JUST SPOOKED YOU BECAUSE YOU DIDN'T KNOW WHAT IT WAS!
CLICK
HAPPY FAMILY!
THEY WERE JUST TALKING AT EACH OTHER--IT'S NOT LIKE THEY HAVE CREEPY CLICK VOICES ON PURPOSE. AND IT WAS KIND OF CUTE!
AND YOU KNOW, PLENTY OF PEOPLE ARE AFRAID OF BATS--BUT THEY EAT THE BUGS AND KEEP DISEASE AT BAY!
WHO'S AFRAID OF BATS? BATS ARE HEROES!
THEY'RE MOSTLY HUNGRY FLYING MAMMALS... BUT THAT'S A PRETTY COOL THING TO BE, AS A HUNGRY, FLYING MAMMAL MYSELF.
YOU DON'T HAVE TO CHANGE ONE THING ABOUT YOURSELF, FRANKIE.
THE ANIMALS IN YOUR FIELD GUIDE AREN'T SCARY BECAUSE THEY'RE BAD--THEY'RE SCARY BECAUSE IT HELPS THEM SURVIVE! THEY'RE JUST TRYING TO LIVE THEIR SPOOKY LIVES!
LIKE ME!!!
YOU BETCHA, MY CREEPY KIDDO.

I AM CREEPY!

AND YOU'RE CUTE! AND COOL! AND SMART! AND CURIOUS AND BRAVE AND I'M VERY VERY PROUD OF YOU!!!

NOW EAT UP, YA CREEPY CUTE CRITTER! OR SHOULD I GET YOU SOME MOSQUITOES?
EWW MOM, YUCK!

ARE YOU SURE? I BET THEY'RE FULL OF PROTEIN! I BET THEY'RE EEEEEEEXTRA CRUNCHY!
NO! THANK YOU! I'LL STICK TO TACOS!

THE NEXT MORNING...
MOSSTOWN ELEMENTARY SCHOOL

UM... YES, FRANKIE?

I'D LIKE TO INTRODUCE MYSELF AGAIN!

OH! WELL....
I BROUGHT A HANDOUT FOR EVERYONE.

TAKE ONE AND PASS IT BACK, PLEASE.
I GUESS THIS IS FINE!!

AHEM.

HI! I'M FRANKIE FAIRY!
IT'S NICE TO MEET YOU AGAIN!
I LIKE NATURE WALKS AND STRAW-BERRIES, AND MY PET WOOLY BEAR, TUNA!
MY MOM AND I JUST MOVED HERE--SHE'S A PROFESSOR AT MOSSTOWN UNIVERSITY!
SHE'S AN EXPERT IN ANIMAL BIOLOGY!
I'M INTERESTED IN THAT TOO!
I LIKE ANIMALS THAT ARE CUTE AND COOL BUT A LITTLE CREEPY... LIKE ME!

MY HOBBY IS MAKING A FIELD GUIDE FOR ALL OF THE PLANTS AND ANIMALS I SEE.

I MADE COPIES FOR ALL OF YOU, IN CASE YOU'D LIKE TO SEE IT TOO!
FRANKIE'S FIELD GUIDE

I ADDED A BIOGRAPHY AT THE END, IF YOU WANT TO LEARN A LITTLE BIT MORE ABOUT ME!
THAT'S IT! IT'S NICE TO MEET YOU ALL!

I HOPE... WE CAN BE FRIENDS....

HI, FRANKIE!

THIS SAYS YOU RODE A POSSUM, IS THAT TRUE?!
I DIDN'T KNOW SNAKES COULD YAWN!
I HAVE A WOOLY BEAR TOO, HIS NAME IS BOB!

YES! AND I FED ONE A STRAW-BERRY!!!
YES, SNAKE YAWNS ARE SUPER CUTE!!! CHECK MY DIAGRAM ON PAGE FIVE!
BOB IS A GREAT NAME FOR A WOOLY BEAR!!!
PSSSH.

YOU REALLY EXPECT US TO BELIEVE ANY OF THIS?
SNAKES *YAWN*? BATS SAVED YOU? POSSUMS EAT STRAWBERRIES??
YOU'RE SCARY **AND** A LIAR.
FIELD GUIDE
FIELD GUIDE

CLICK
CLICK
CLICK

WHOA!!! SEE? LIKE I SAID, SCARY!
FIELD GUIDE

FRANKIE, PLEASE, WE DON'T CLICK IN THE CLASS-ROOM!!
CLICK CLIC

CLACK

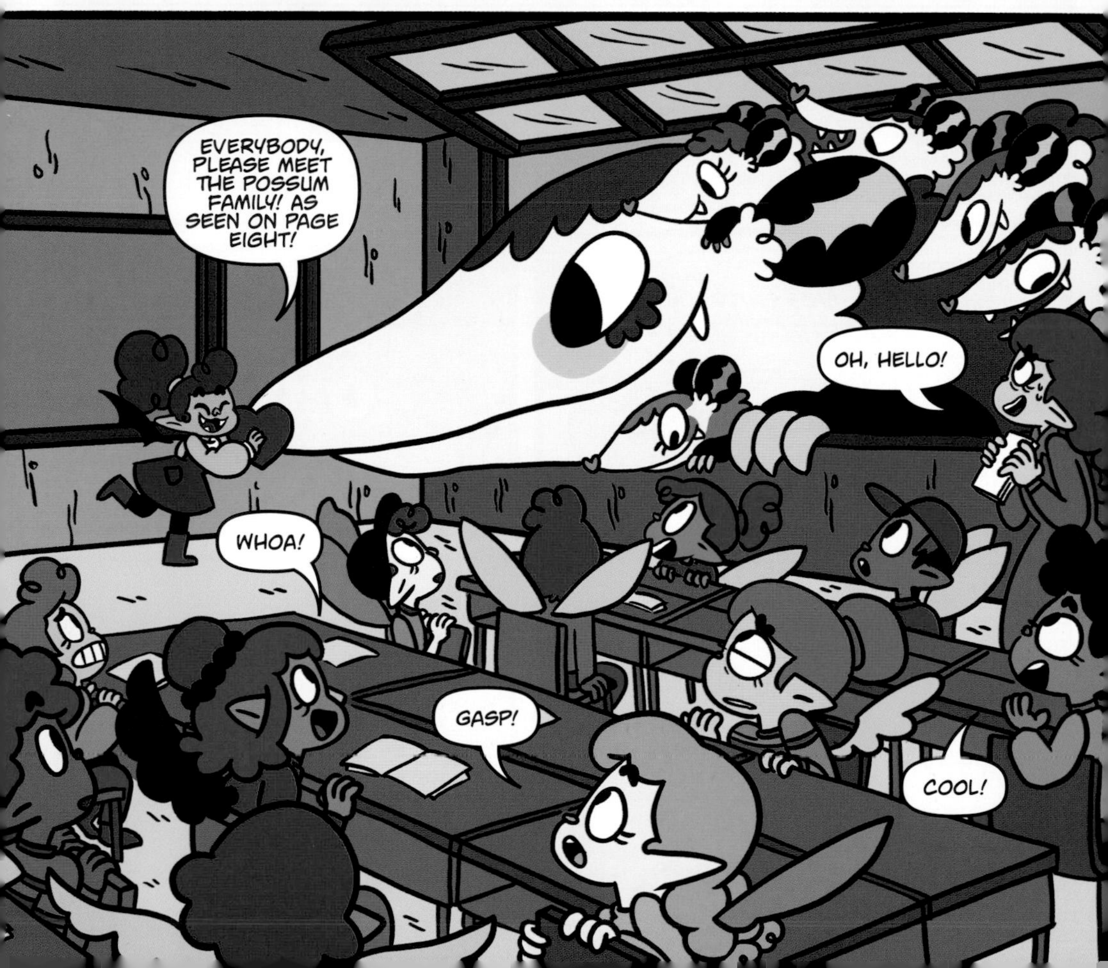
EVERYBODY, PLEASE MEET THE POSSUM FAMILY! AS SEEN ON PAGE EIGHT!
OH, HELLO!
WHOA!
GASP!
COOL!

CLACK

FRANKIE "SCARY" FAIRY

YOU TELL 'EM, MOMMA POSSUM!

BIG HAIR

POINTY TEETH

COOL BAT WINGS

MY FIELD GUIDE

"TUNA"

• OMNIVOROUS
• FRIENDLY

I WANT TO LEARN ABOUT CRITTERS THAT ARE CREEPY AND CUTE ... JUST LIKE ME!

THE END!

FRANKIE SAYS
I'M A FAIRY, SO THE RULES ARE A LITTLE DIFFERENT FOR ME--BUT MAKE SURE YOU GIVE THESE ANIMALS SPACE IF YOU SEE THEM IN REAL LIFE!
NEVER TOUCH A WILD ANIMAL--YOU HAVE TO LET THEM LIVE THEIR SPOOKY LITTLE LIVES, TOO!
WRITE YOUR FIELD GUIDE FROM A DISTANCE! ADMIRE ANIMALS FROM AFAR!
SNAKES
GO TO YOUR LOCAL LIBRARY TO FIND OUT MORE ABOUT COMMON GARTER SNAKES, NORTH AMERICAN OPOSSUMS, MOSQUITOES, AND LITTLE BROWN BATS.
UNTIL NEXT TIME, STAY **SAFE**--AND CUTE N' CREEPY!
FRANKIE

CAITLIN ROSE BOYLE

grew up admiring all sorts of creepy critters in rural southern Maryland. When she isn't drawing comics, she's working as a storyboard revisionist in the animation industry. She lives in Los Angeles, CA with an extensive collection of houseplants.

DEWDROP
By Katie O'Neill

BOOGER BEARD
By Vicente "Vinny" Navarrete

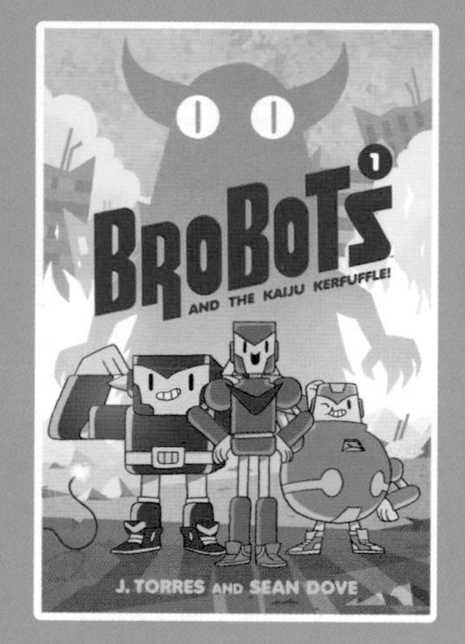

BROBOTS AND THE KAIJU KERFUFFLE
By J. Torres and Sean Dove

FAST ENOUGH: BESSIE STRINGFIELD'S FIRST RIDE
By Joel Christian Gill

MORE GREAT READS FROM ONI-LION FORGE!